S0-EDN-065

FOR LALA AND MY LALA MUMMY — T.K.

FOR EMILY AND HER BIRDS — C.C.

Text copyright © 2022 by Thomas King
Illustrations copyright © 2022 by Charlene Chua

Tundra Books, an imprint of Tundra Book Group,
a division of Penguin Random House of Canada Limited

All rights reserved. The use of any part of this publication reproduced, transmitted in any form or by any means, electronic, mechanical, photocopying, recording, or otherwise, or stored in a retrieval system, without the prior written consent of the publisher — or, in case of photocopying or other reprographic copying, a licence from the Canadian Copyright Licensing Agency — is an infringement of the copyright law.

Library and Archives Canada Cataloguing in Publication

Title: My Lala / Thomas King ; illustrated by Charlene Chua.
Names: King, Thomas, 1943- author. | Chua, Charlene, illustrator.
Identifiers: Canadiana (print) 20210181451 | Canadiana (ebook) 2021018146X |
ISBN 9780735269347 (hardcover) | ISBN 9780735269354 (EPUB) | ISBN 9781774883754 (special markets)
Classification: LCC PS8571.I5298 M93 2022 | DDC jC813/.54—dc23

Published simultaneously in the United States of America by Tundra Books of Northern New York,
an imprint of Tundra Book Group, a division of Penguin Random House of Canada Limited

Library of Congress Control Number: 2021936257

Acquired by Tara Walker
Edited by Peter Phillips
Designed by Emma Dolan
The artwork in this book was rendered in Photoshop.
The text was set in Houserama and Minion Pro.

Printed in China

www.penguinrandomhouse.ca

2   3   4   5   27   26   25   24   23

MY LALA

Words by
Thomas King

Pictures by
Charlene Chua

tundra

One morning, when morning came bright as a pearl,
Lala decided that she owned the world.

So, out of bed, out of bed, quick as a fox

to My Lala closet and My Lala box.

Now, My Lala box with its My Lala drawers
was a shimmering shimmer of treasures galore.

There were My Lala ribbons and My Lala bows,
my Lala feather that fell off a crow.

My Lala candy
all sugary yummy
hid-hidden away
from My Lala's mummy.

My Lala hairbrush all tangled with knots
and a plasticky package of shiny red dots.

"**MY LALA DOTS!**" Lala shouted with glee.
"I'll stick these red dots on whatever I see.

So, off I go, off I go, quick at a trot
to mark what is mine, 'cause there's nothing that's not."

"Here's a shiny red dot for My Lala bear,
who doesn't complain when I trim-trim her hair.

One for My Lala blankie and My Lala book
and My Lala raincoat that hangs on a hook."

"One for My Lala boots
that I wear when there's snow

and My Lala jacket,
when winter winds blow.

Here's dots for the markers I use to make scrawls
in My Lala bedroom on My Lala walls."

"I'll put My Lala dots on My Lala hat
that I tape to the head of My Lala cat.

And on My Lala penguin and My Lala sheep,
who snuggle beside me whenever I sleep."

But when Lala put dots on dad-daddy's socks,
she discovered there were no more dots in the box.

"EGAD!" shouted Lala. "This cannot be true! I must have red dots! Oh, what will I do?"

Then skippy-step, skippy-step, back to the drawers
with their My Lala shimmer of treasures galore.

Here's My Lala paper and My Lala glue
and My Lala scissors to cut things in two.

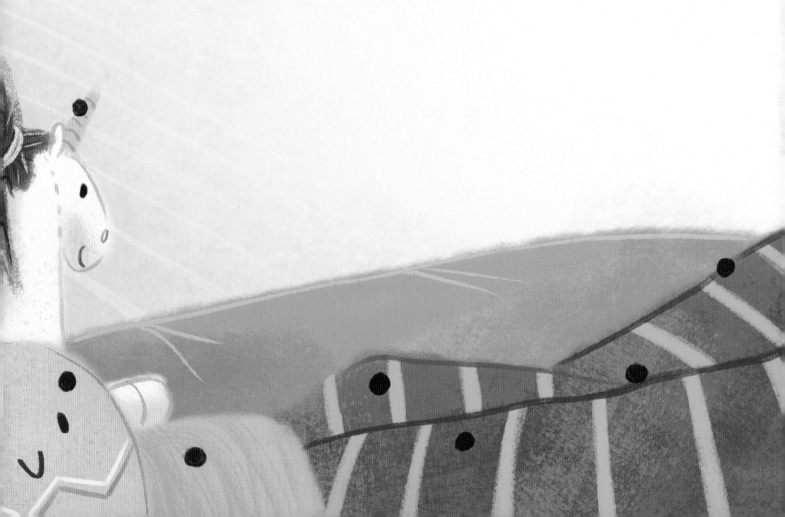

So, all of that day Lala sat on her bed
snip-snipping more dots and painting them red . . .

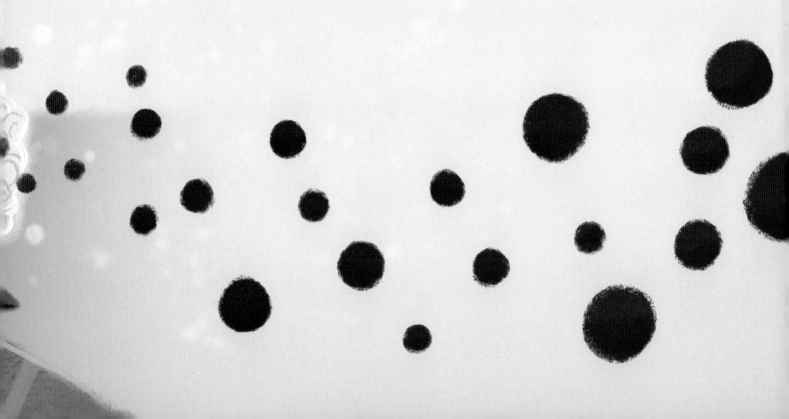

. . . till My Lala room was filled ceiling to floor
with My Lala dots, and **SHE**

KEPT

MAKING

MORE.

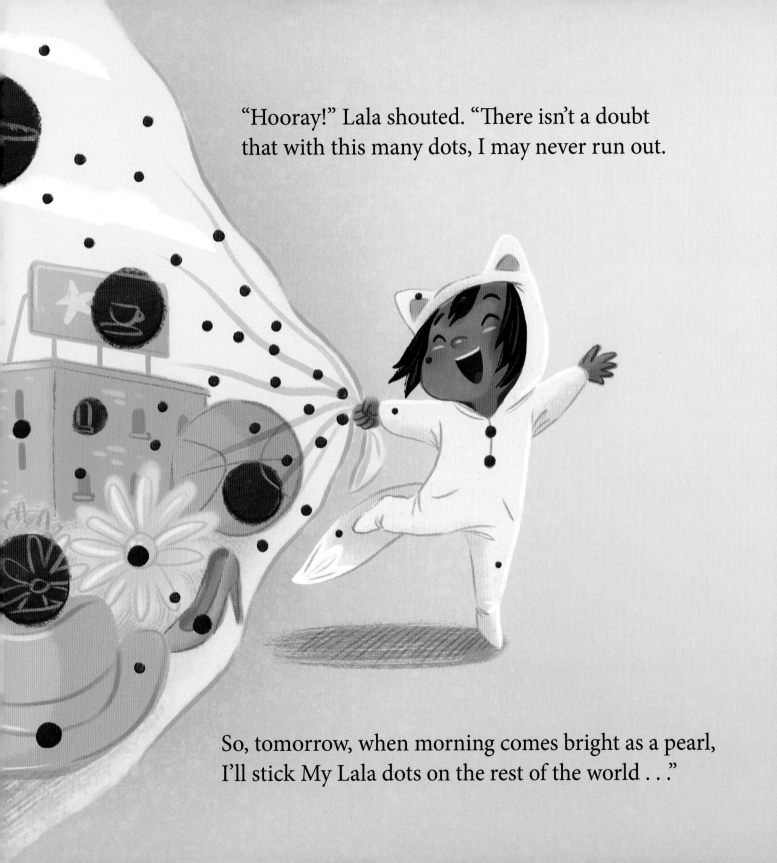

"Hooray!" Lala shouted. "There isn't a doubt
that with this many dots, I may never run out.

So, tomorrow, when morning comes bright as a pearl,
I'll stick My Lala dots on the rest of the world . . ."

"... no matter the weather, no matter the time.

'Cause my name is **LALA.**

MY NAME IS **LALA.**

MY NAME IS **LALA**
AND
ALL THIS
IS **MINE!**"